The Dog and the

An Aesop's Fable

retold by Cynthia Swain
illustrated by Joanna Czernichowska

It was a hard winter, and every day was bitter cold in the forest. The birds flew south to escape the chill. Many animals were hibernating, or sleeping for the winter.

Wolf did not hibernate. He was wide-awake. At first, Wolf liked winter. The woods grew quiet after the birds flew south. Many animals stayed in their burrows or caves. Wolf had the whole forest to himself.

Wolf ran freely through the trees. He jumped in the snow and slid across frozen ponds.

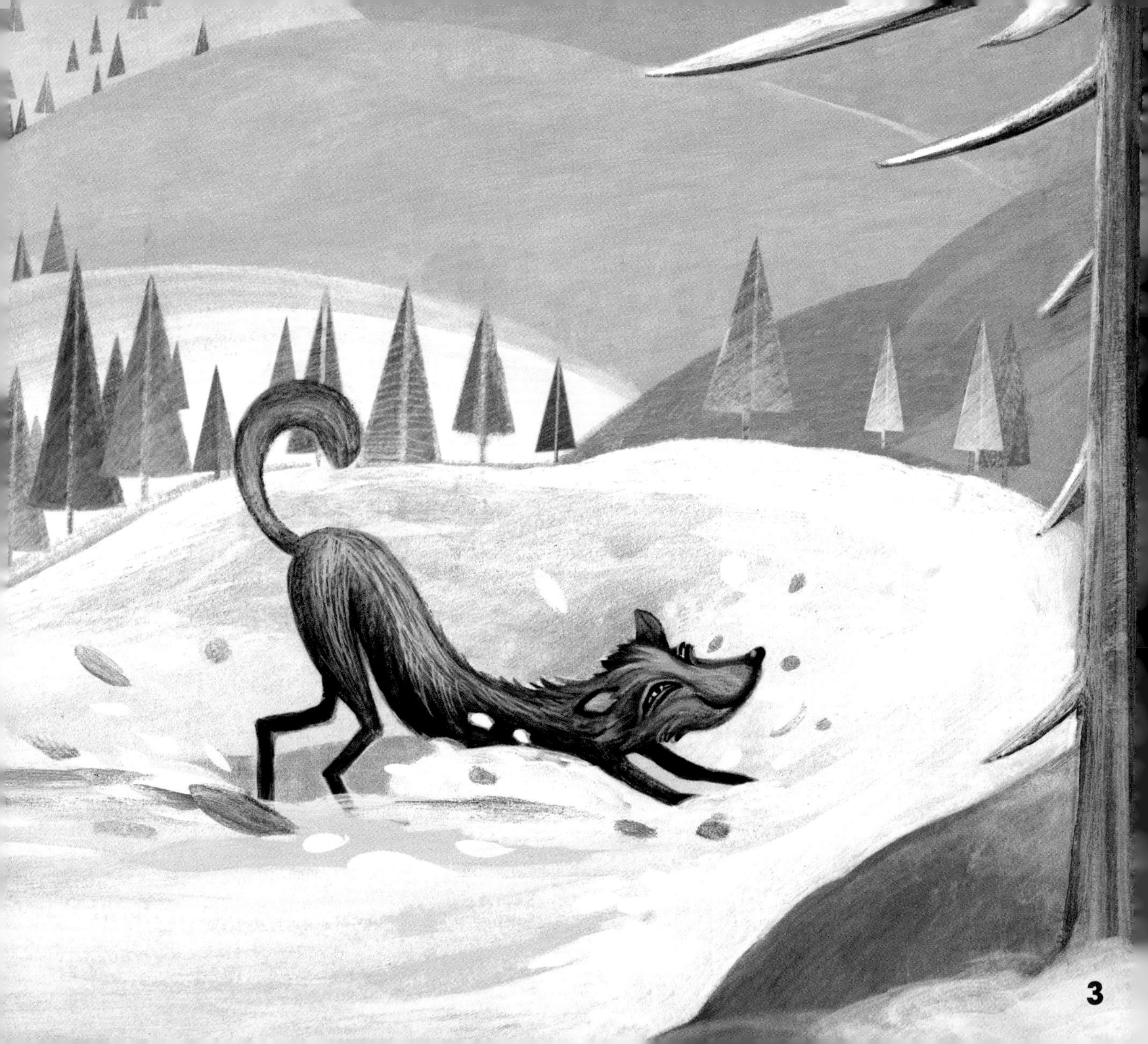

But soon the snow piled high on the forest floor. Wolf found it hard to find food. He grew hungry and tired and weak. His ribs showed through the skin on his slender body.

"Ow-woo! Ow-woo!" he howled. His cry in the night could be heard as far away as the farms.

"Woof! Woof!" barked a reply.

Wolf was surprised. "Gee, that sounds like the bark of my cousin, Dog," he said. "I haven't seen him in ages. I will call to him. Maybe he will help me."

Wolf used the last of his strength and made a long, sad cry. "Oww! Oww!"

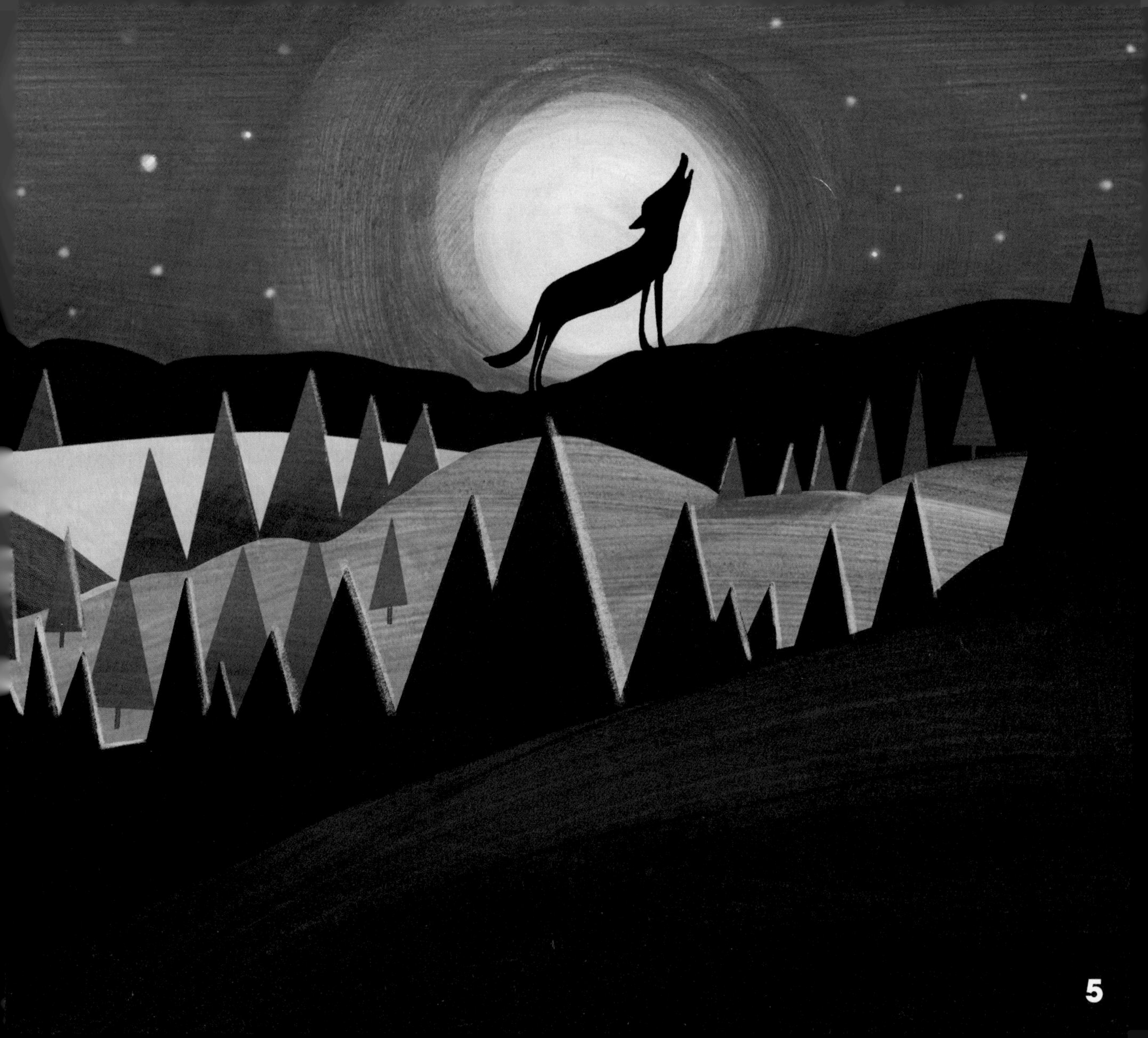

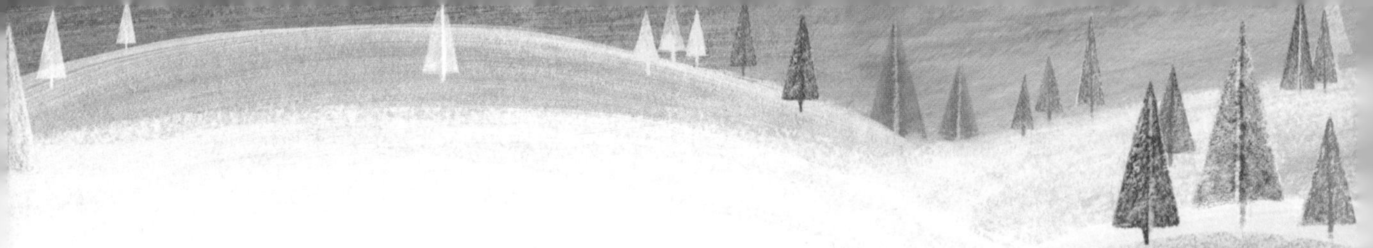

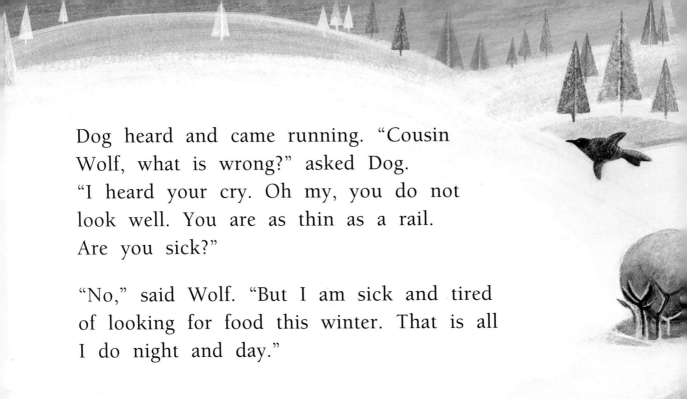

Dog heard and came running. "Cousin Wolf, what is wrong?" asked Dog. "I heard your cry. Oh my, you do not look well. You are as thin as a rail. Are you sick?"

"No," said Wolf. "But I am sick and tired of looking for food this winter. That is all I do night and day."

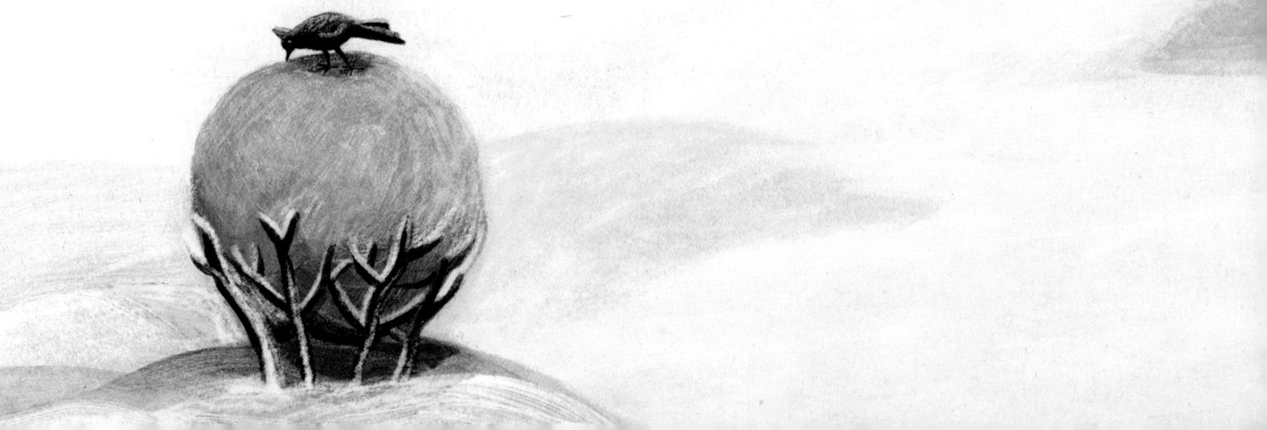

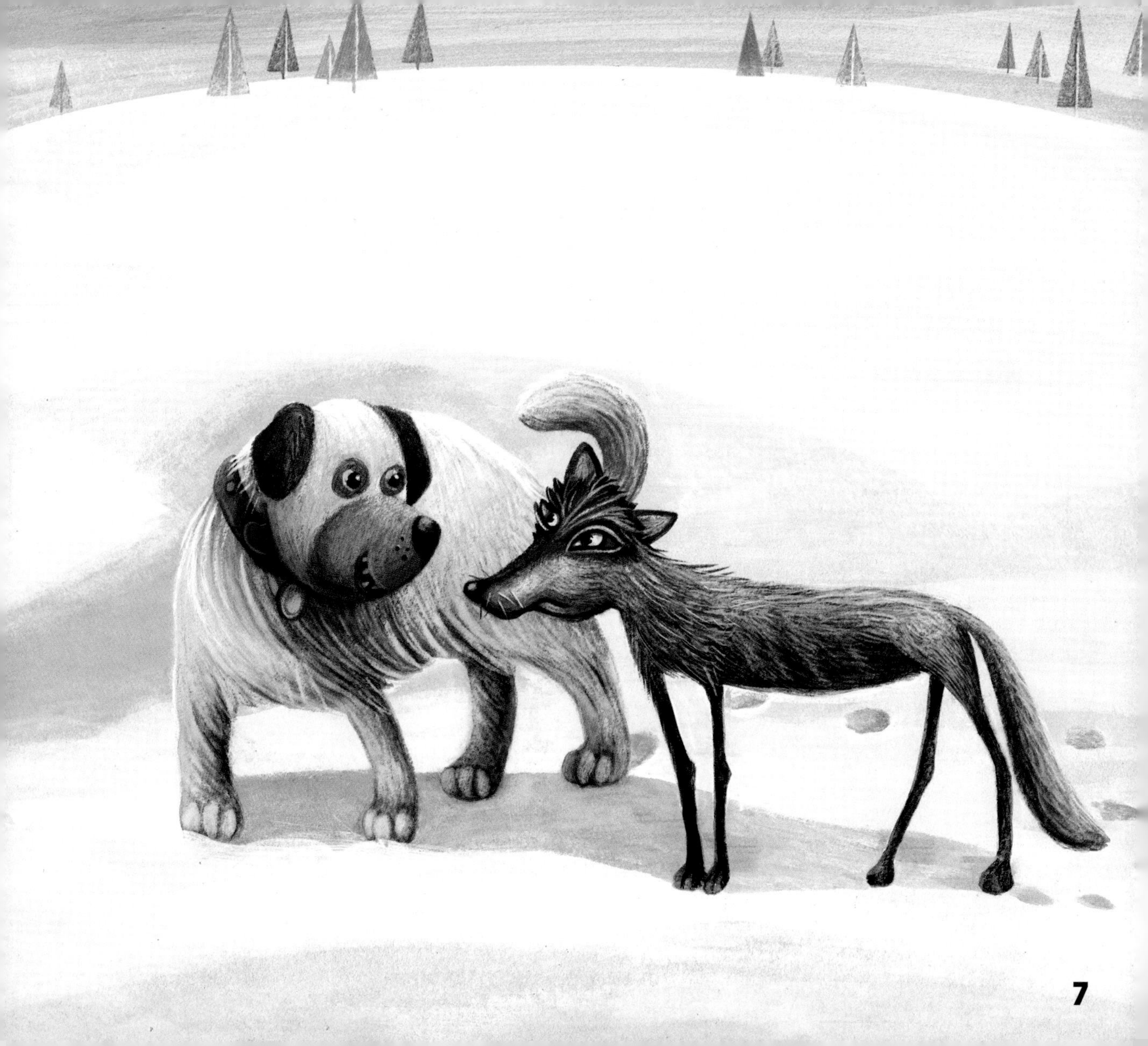

“I can help you,” exclaimed Dog. “Come and live with me on the farm. Work a little and you will get a lot to eat, twice a day. It’s a wonderful life!”

“Hmm,” Wolf thought. “Will your master let me stay?” he asked.

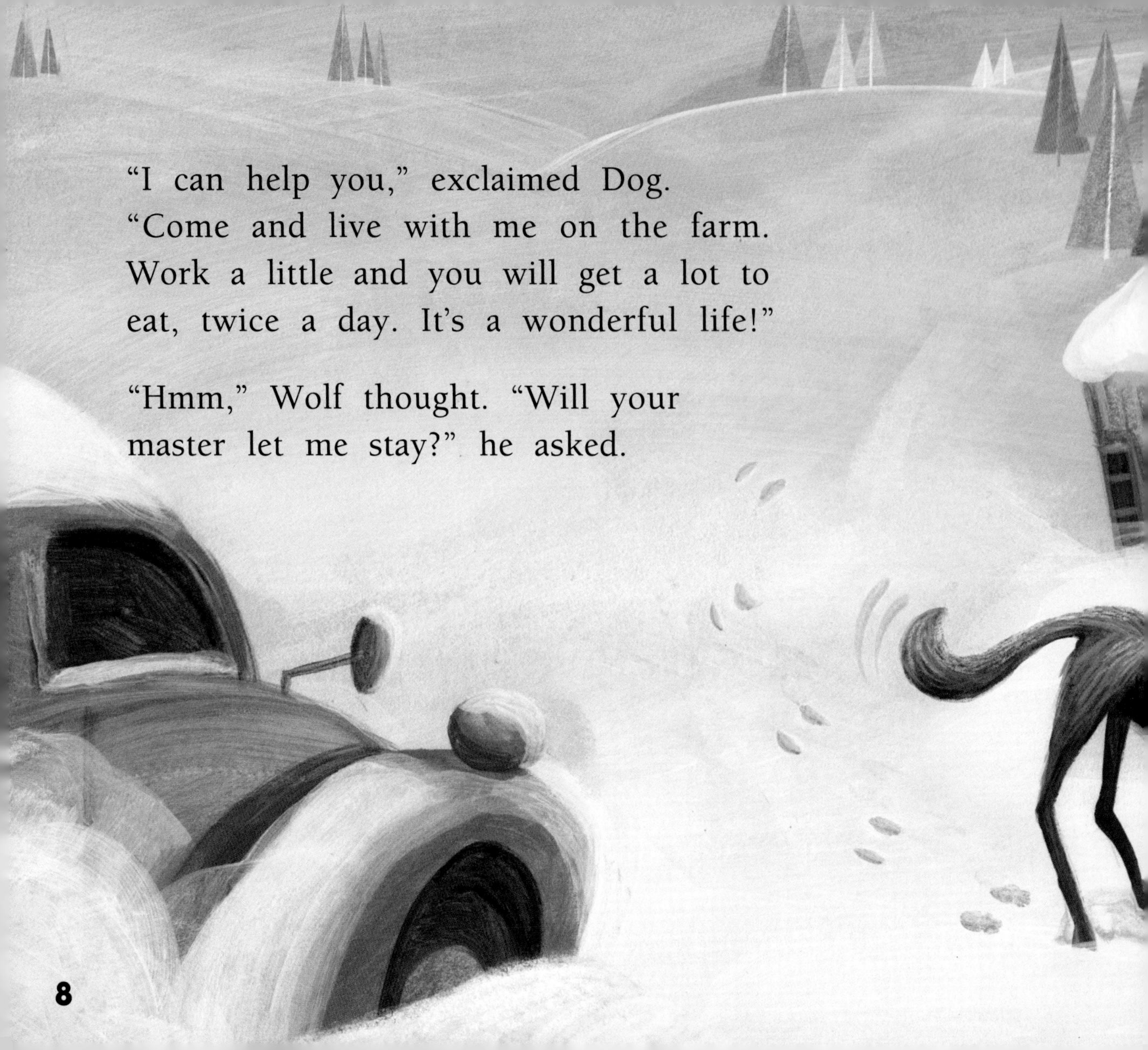

"My master needs many animals to help him with many chores," answered Dog. "I will tell my master you will be a great addition to the group. I'll tell him you will work your tail off."

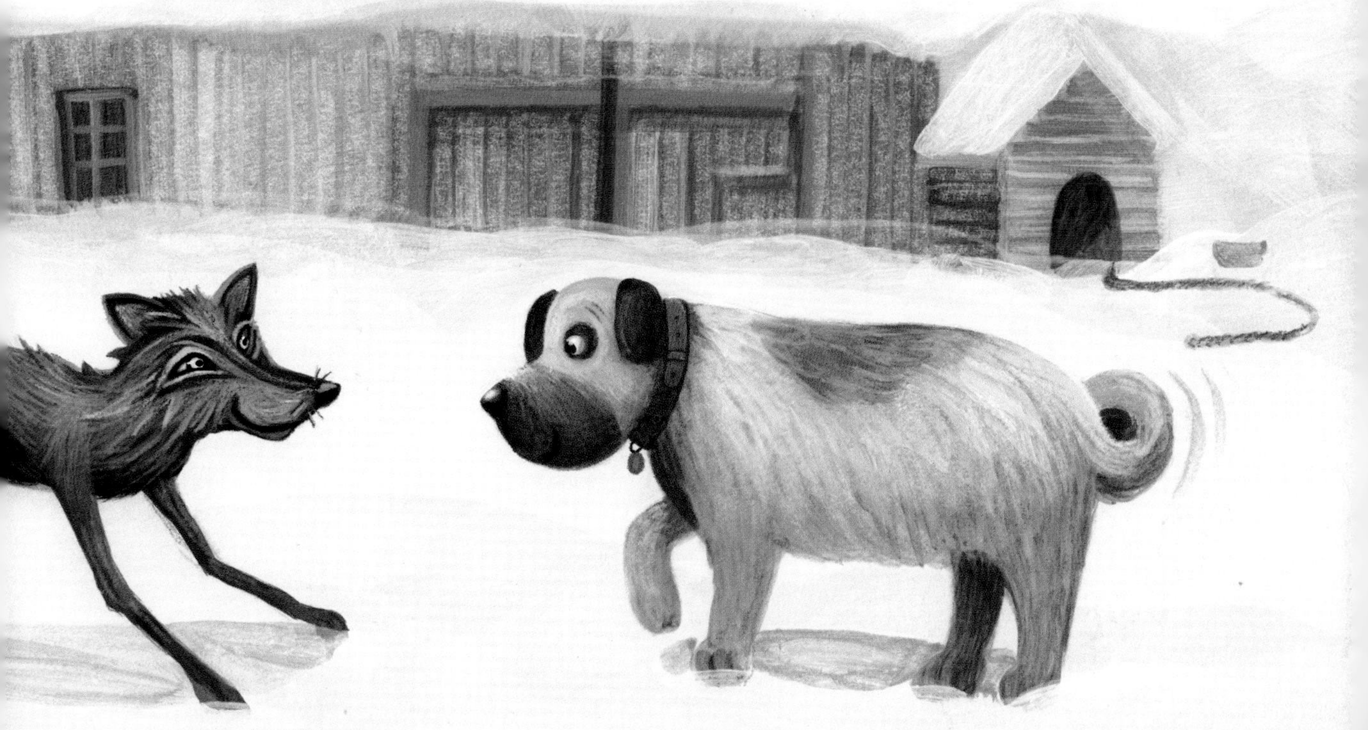

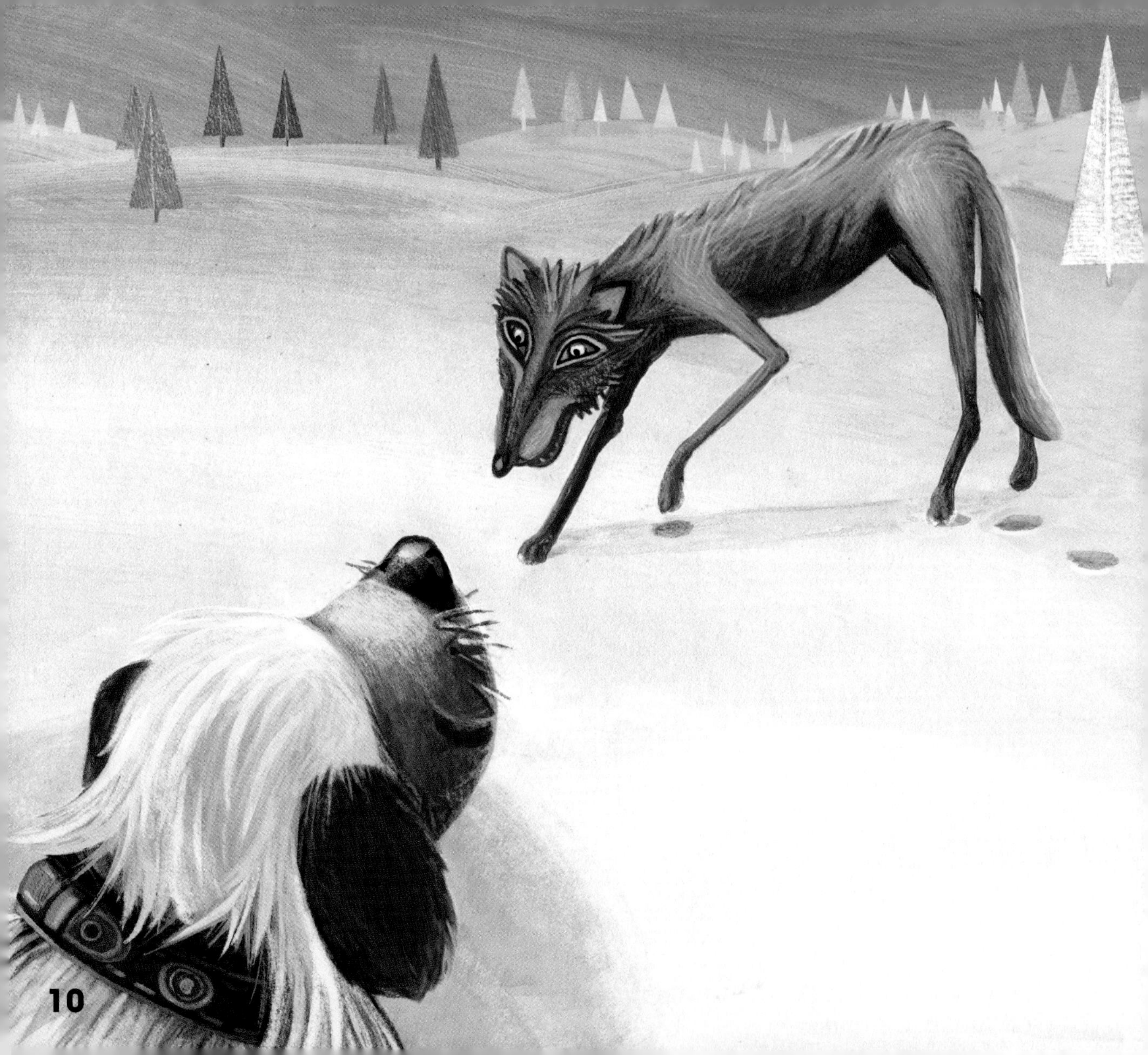

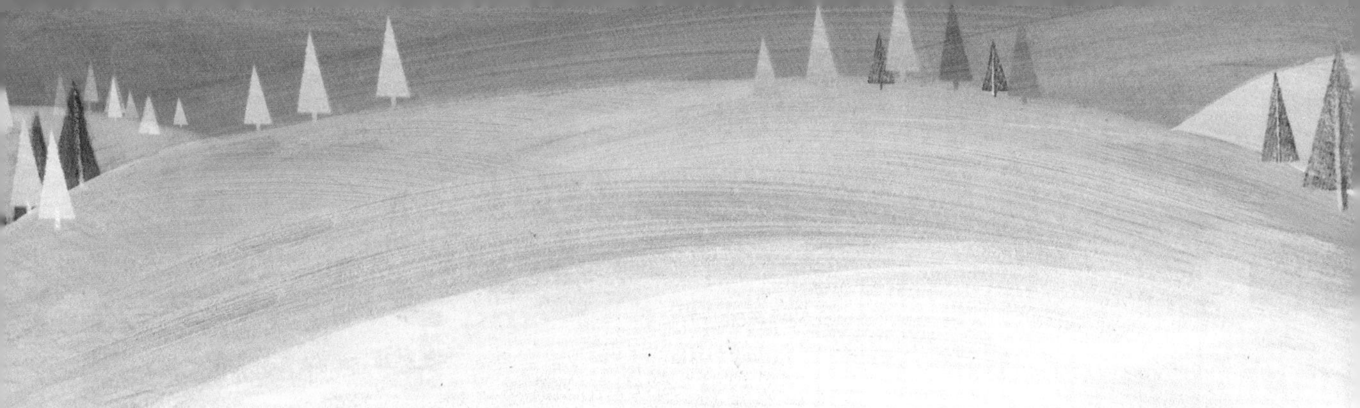

Wolf was so happy he was on top of the world.
He would have a job, and he would have food.
Then Dog told Wolf about the work. For example,
Dog helped his master hunt for game.

Wolf said, "I am an expert hunter. I can find
any wild animals in the forest. This job will
be a piece of cake for me."

As Wolf and Dog walked along, Wolf noticed that Dog was wearing a collar.

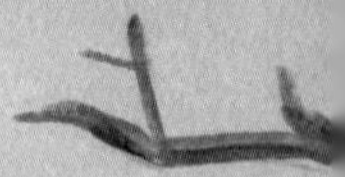

"Tell me, Cousin," Wolf said, "what is that around your neck?"

"Oh, that? It's nothing," said Dog. "My master keeps a collar on me, and he chains me up at night. In fact, I need to return before he finds out I'm gone. I'm used to the collar now. You'll get used to it."

Wolf was horrified.

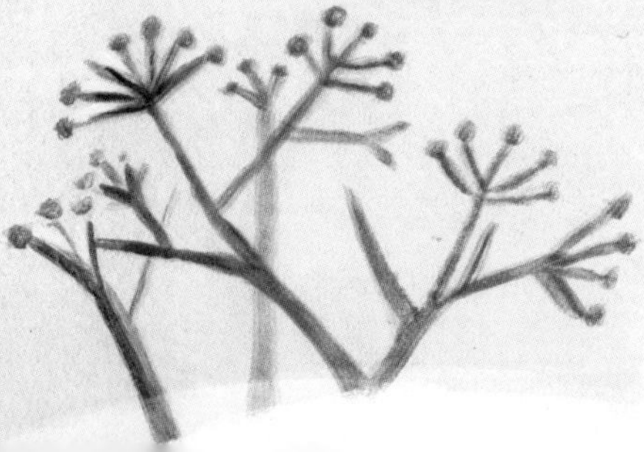

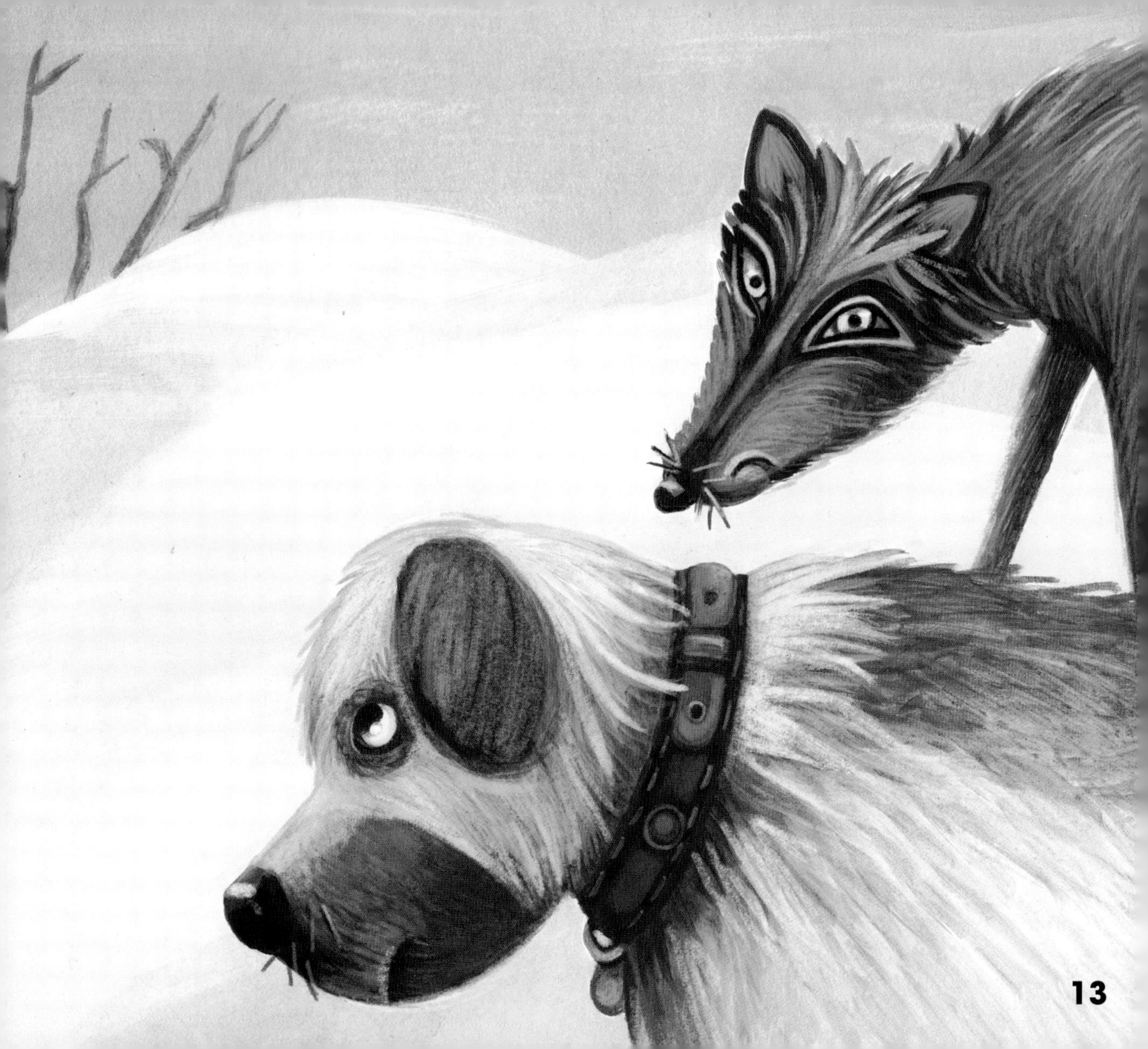

"A collar? Chains? Oh no, cousin Dog," sputtered Wolf. "I don't think I could ever grow used to that. I cannot survive that way. I was born to be free. I'd rather starve than be tied down."

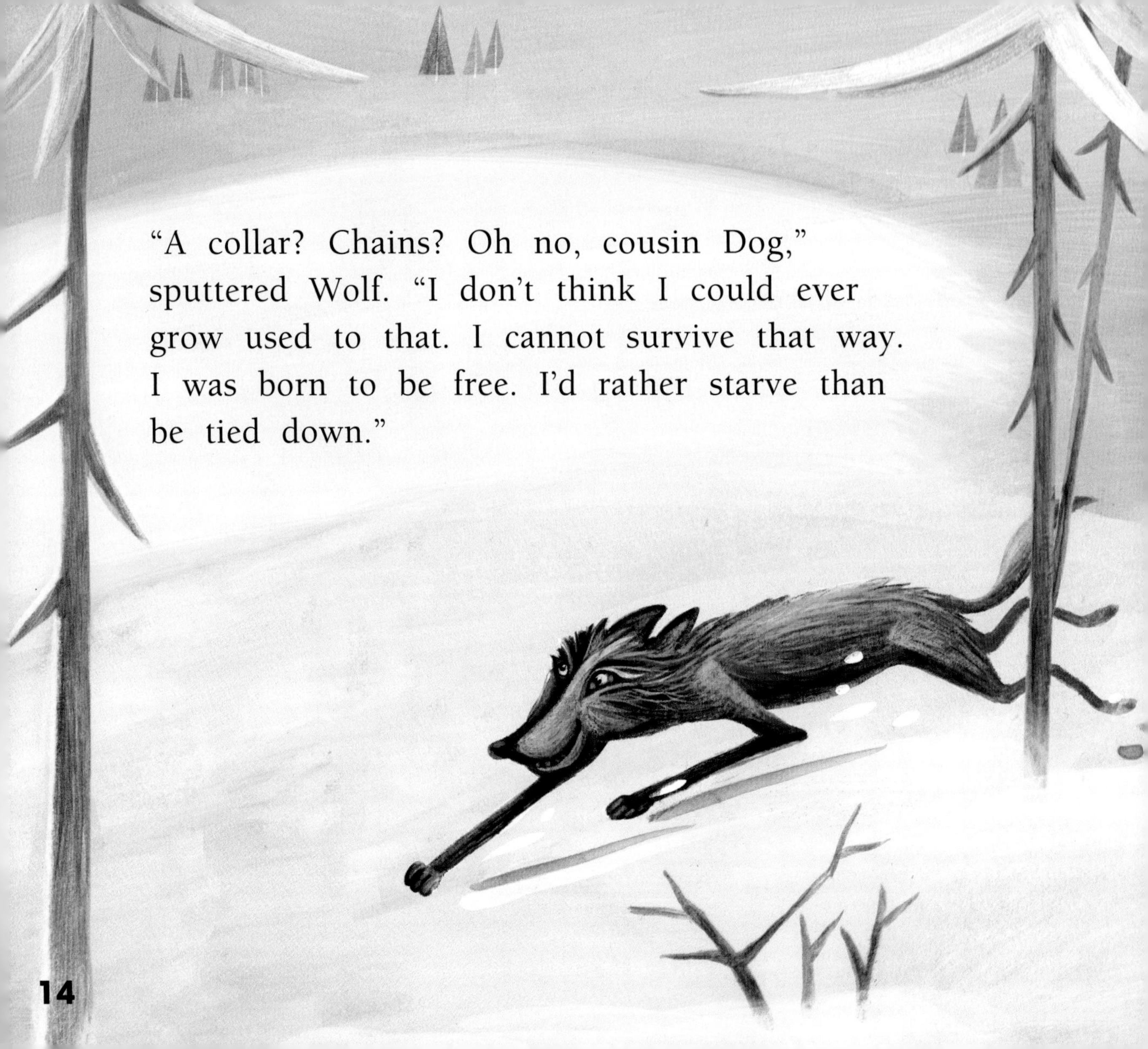

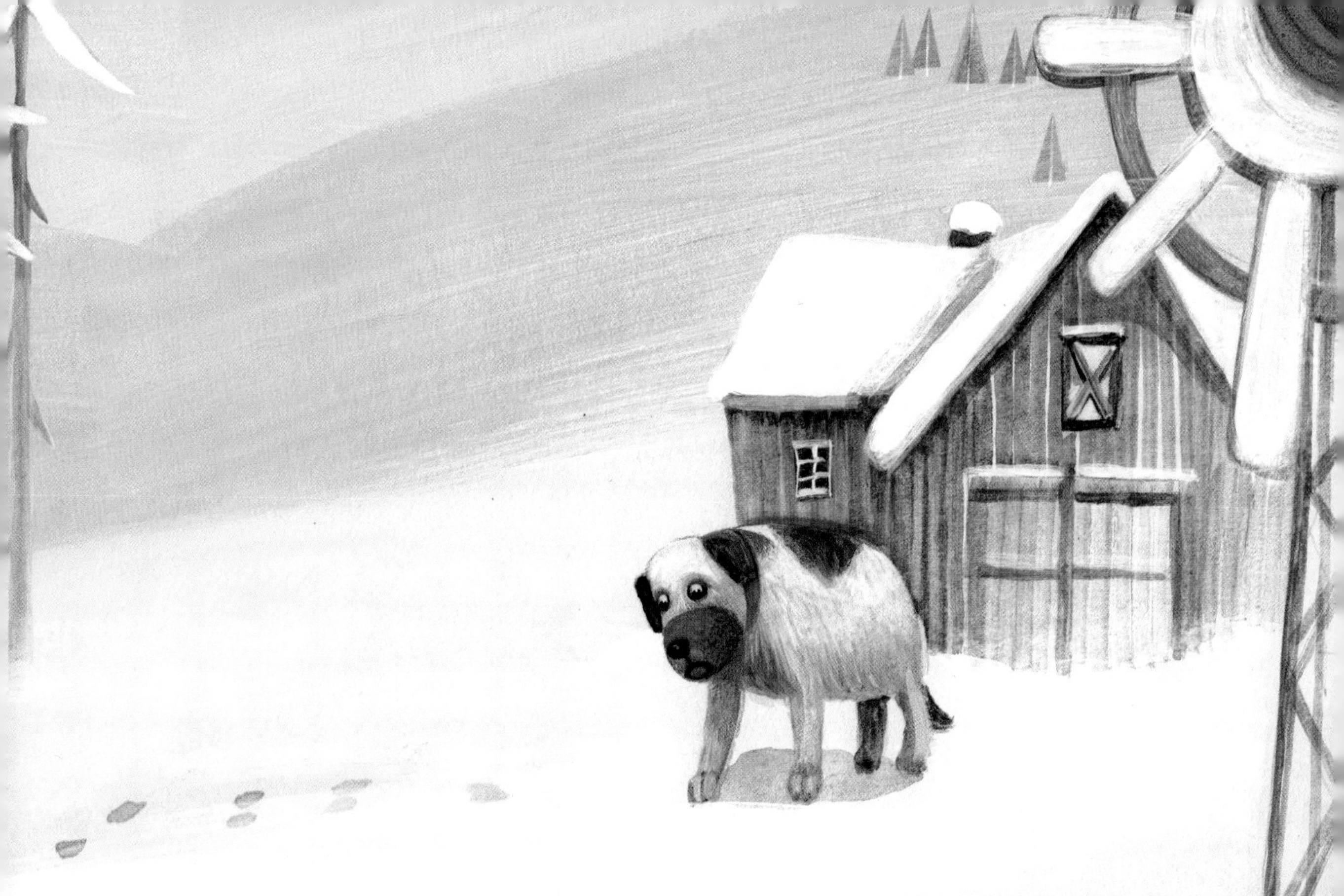

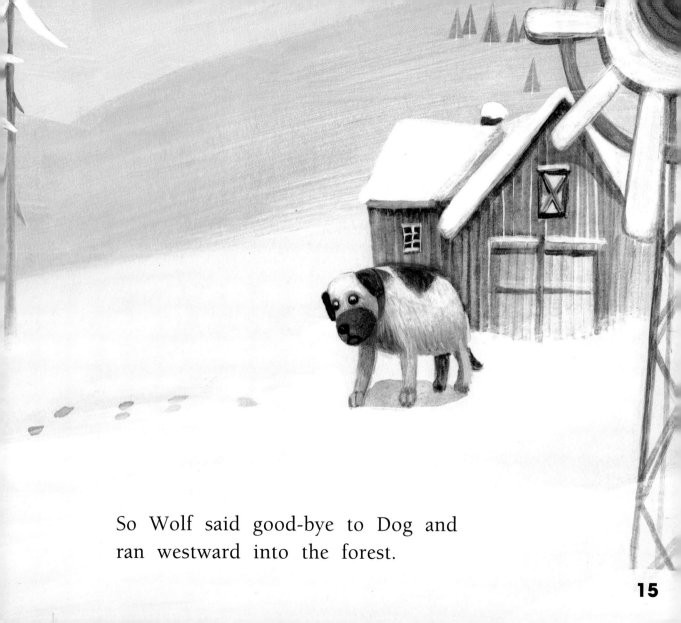

So Wolf said good-bye to Dog and
ran westward into the forest.

He was a free wolf, and
a free wolf he would stay!

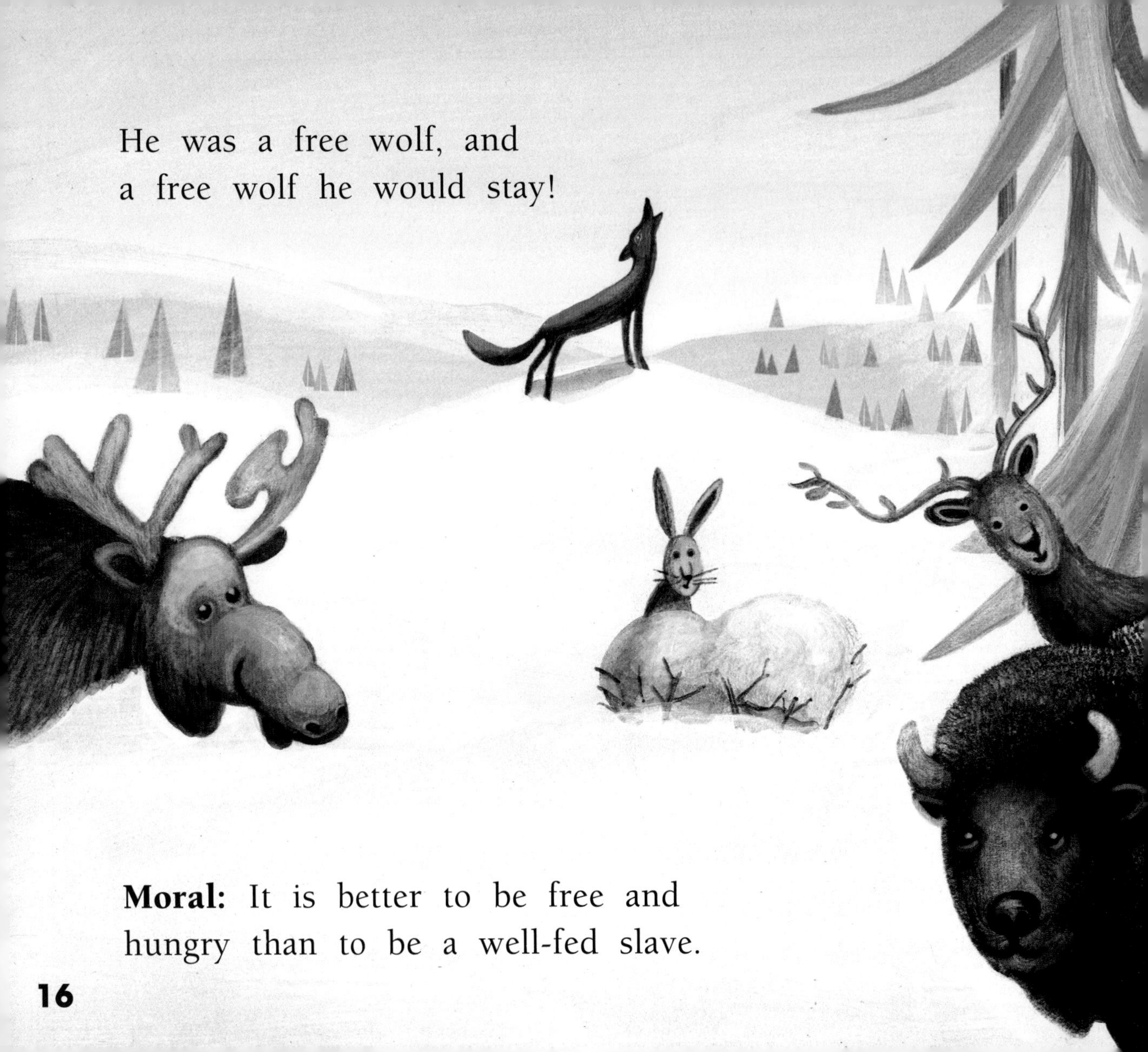

Moral: It is better to be free and hungry than to be a well-fed slave.